MORE BOOKS ABOUT JAMES BOND JR

FROM MAMMOTH:
As Good As Gold
In this adventure game book, you face the risks, make the choices — and face the consequences — as James Bond Junior travels to Egypt to stop Goldfinger and his evil henchman, Odd Job, from succeeding in their latest dastardly plot!

FROM BUZZ BOOKS:
Tunnel of Doom
James and his friends must prevent the mad Dr Derange and his loyal helper, Skullcap, from destroying Scotland Yard...

Barbella's Revenge
James and I.Q. follow Nick Nack to Brazil, where they uncover Barbella's scheme to take over control of S.C.U.M...

Freeze Frame
When there's a blizzard in the middle of summer, James and I.Q. find that all the clues to the mystery lead to Goldfinger and Odd Job...

Dangerous Games
James and his friends become involved in a perilous war game when Baron Von Skarin takes over a tropical island with lethal toy weapons...

First published in Great Britain 1993 by Mammoth
an imprint of Mandarin Paperbacks
Reed International Books Limited
Michelin House, 81 Fulham Road, London SW3 6RB
and Auckland, Melbourne, Singapore and Toronto

Reprinted 1993

ISBN 0 7497 1354 2

A CIP catalogue record for this book is available at the British Library.

Printed at Cox and Wyman,
Cardiff Road, Reading

JAMES BOND JR™

SPY FILE

Clare Dannatt

Illustrations by
SPJ Design Consultants

MAMMOTH

'My name is Bond... James Bond Junior'

Introducing James Bond Junior! His uncle is secret agent, James Bond, otherwise known as 007. Bond Junior has inherited the brains, style and adventurous spirit of 007. He's a typical teenager - with one exception - James' favourite hobby is cracking international crime capers. At seventeen, James Bond Junior is ready for a slice of the action.

James and his friends pit their wits against the deadly organisation S.C.U.M. (Saboteurs and Criminals United in Mayhem) in hair-raising adventures that take them all over the world. James has to evade not only the evil S.C.U.M. agents - but school authorities as well! His objective is to bust the criminals in time to get back to his lessons without being 'busted' himself. When it comes to seeing justice done, James Bond Junior doesn't let a few rules and regulations stand in his way.

School for Spies

James is a student at Warfield Academy. Nestled deep in the countryside on the south coast of England, Warfield Academy is a high-security boarding school for the offspring of political leaders, diplomats and espionage agents from all over the world. It's surrounded by a high wall, and guarded day and night by security staff and video cameras. All of this security is meant to protect the pupils, but for James Bond Junior, the main problem is getting in and out on his missions without getting caught!

A C A D E M Y

Term Report

Student:	James Bond Junior
Mathematics	James enjoys solving difficult problems.
Science	Has a good general knowledge of science, but rushes experiments in order to find a solution.
English	James is creative and enjoys reading, but should perhaps read fewer comics.
Languages	James is obviously at ease in foreign lands.
Physical Education	James is well-coordinated and has made flying leaps this term.
General Conduct	He is a good scholar, and would be a credit to the academy were it not for his perpetual flaunting of Warfield rules and his out-of-school activities.

We're right behind you, James!

Horace 'I.Q.' Boothroyd

James shares a room at Warfield with I.Q., whose ingenious inventions are sometimes lifesavers. His grandfather, Q, works with 007.

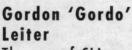

Gordon 'Gordo' Leiter

The son of CIA agent Felix Leiter, Gordo is a radical American dude and a good friend to James.

Tracy Milbanks

As the headmaster's daughter, Tracy should set an example for the others, but she'd rather help James on his missions.

Buddy Mitchell

Buddy teaches PE at Warfield Academy and trains James in the martial arts and gymnastics. He once worked for the FBI (Federal Bureau of Investigation).

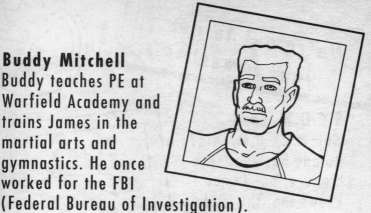

Trevor Noseworthy

The son of an English earl, Trevor is forever trying to get James into trouble. Behind Trevor's snooty facade, James can see that he is really just eager to join the crowd.

Phoebe Farragut

Phoebe's parents are fabulously wealthy, and her credit cards come in handy when James needs funds for his missions. Luckily, Phoebe is both loyal and generous.

We're out to get you, James!

S.C.U.M. Lord
Who is S.C.U.M. Lord?
No one has ever seen
his face, but James
knows that this evil
shadowy figure
gives the orders to
S.C.U.M. agents.

Jaws
Jaws is the towering 2.3
metre-high giant with the
steely teeth. It's bad news
for James when he sees
that metal grin lighting
up a dark night!

Nick Nack
You don't have to be tall
to be S.C.U.M. Nick
Nack is only 1.2 metres
tall, but he's full of
wicked little tricks.

Barbella
This iron lady does bench-presses for fun. She'd like to take over S.C.U.M. Lord's power - but she's got more brawn than brain.

Captain Walker D. Plank
Somewhere beneath the South Pacific ocean skulks Captain Walker D. Plank in his undersea empire. From there he controls his high-tech pirate ships.

Tiara Hotstones
Jewels are Tiara's passion, and she loves stealing them. In fact, Hotstones is known throughout the criminal world as the greatest cat burglar in the business.

Cracking the code

An important skill for
any spy is decoding secret messages. The best
codebreaker around Warfield is I.Q., of course.

THE MORSE CODE

Morse code was invented in the 1800s by an
American called Samuel Morse. He gave each
letter of the alphabet a different combination
of short and/or long sounds or light flashes.
For example:
'S.O.S.' is 3 short/3 long/3 short signals.

Try sending messages to a friend using
Morse code. Stand on different sides of a
thin wall and tap on the wall, or transmit
light signals with a torch. Copy the chart
here so you and your friend can both
refer to it. Remember to pause
between each letter.

INVISIBLE WRITING

A good way to send a secret message is to make it invisible. All you need is a lemon, a paint brush and paper.

Squeeze some lemon juice into a cup, then dip your brush into the juice and write your message onto the paper. As the message dries, it will disappear.

To read the message, ask an adult to put it under the grill for you for 10 minutes. Make sure that the paper is weighed down at the edges so that it won't burn. Or, you can hold the paper near a light bulb, but this will take a bit longer to work. The heat will make your message visible.

Remember: Spies don't take chances, so let an adult help you.

MINT AMPLIFIER
Why chew a mint when you can listen to it? By putting I.Q.'s special roll of mints up to his ear, James can hear through walls and doors.

SUPER-STICK PADS
By using I.Q.'s super-stick pads, the intrepid James has the nerve to climb up any building - or climb down if he's in a sticky situation!

ULTRA-SOUND BINOCULARS
With these high-tech binoculars, James can distract his enemies with a high-pitched piercing sound while he spies on them.

14

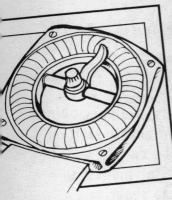

ELECTRO-MAGNETIC BELT BUCKLE

In I.Q.'s hands an ordinary belt buckle becomes a powerful electro-magnet, allowing James to attract and repel metal with a flick of a switch.

SHORTWAVE RADIO-WATCH

This amazing gadget not only tells the time, but is a fully operational short-wave radio. James can either eavesdrop on S.C.U.M. or listen to the latest pop charts.

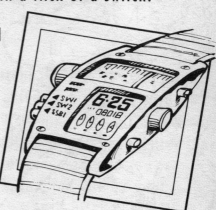

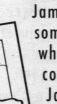

MINI PARACHUTE

James always aims high - sometimes too high! That's when I.Q.'s mini parachute comes in handy to bring James safely back down to earth.

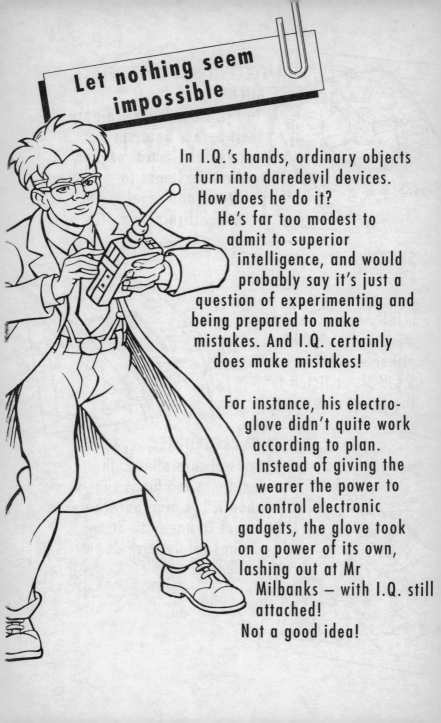

Let nothing seem impossible

In I.Q.'s hands, ordinary objects turn into daredevil devices. How does he do it?

He's far too modest to admit to superior intelligence, and would probably say it's just a question of experimenting and being prepared to make mistakes. And I.Q. certainly does make mistakes!

For instance, his electro-glove didn't quite work according to plan. Instead of giving the wearer the power to control electronic gadgets, the glove took on a power of its own, lashing out at Mr Milbanks — with I.Q. still attached!

Not a good idea!

What kinds of gadgets would be useful to you? Think about new and exciting possibilities for everyday objects. How about a PEN that does homework? A hovercraft TEAPOT? A WASTE BIN that picks up rubbish?

The Spy Telephone

You need: 2 empty yoghurt pots and a piece of string 4 metres long. Make a hole in the bottom of each pot. Thread the ends of the string through the holes and tie a knot in each end to hold the string in place. Give one pot to a friend and stand far away from each other so that the string is taut. While you speak into your pot, your friend can listen through the other pot.

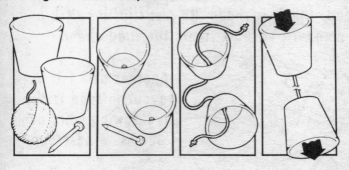

James' Passion for CARS

Cars are as crucial for James Bond Junior as they are for his uncle 007. James has a nippy red sports car crammed with gadgets.

- A TV screen monitor enables James to follow the signals of I.Q.'s specially made homing devices.

- When the S.C.U.M. van scatters tacks in the road, James is ready. He just flips a switch and a magnetic vacuum clears the road ahead.

- Another of S.C.U.M.'s favourite road tricks is throwing paint over James' windscreen.

But James easily activates special spray jets which send paint-removing fluid over the glass.

- When the car is held up at traffic lights, all James has to do is push another control on the dashboard, and a small antenna on the car roof sends out signals that instantly change the lights from red to green!

-James can even drive upside down in tunnels with I.Q.'s incredible sure-grip tyres, loaded with a thousand retractable steel hooks.

Although the Warfield van is usually used for school trips, sometimes James persuades Coach Mitchell to lend him the van keys. In an emergency, James can activate the flight mode to get out of a tight spot.

The Bond-Mobile

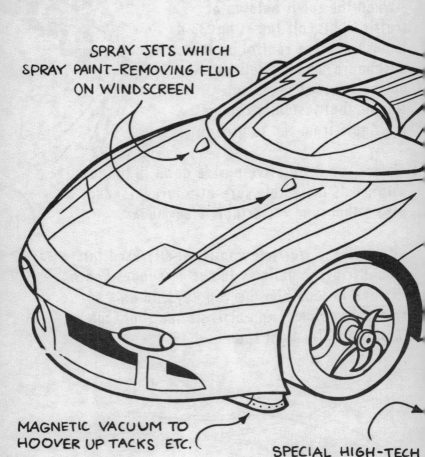

SPRAY JETS WHICH
SPRAY PAINT-REMOVING FLUID
ON WINDSCREEN

MAGNETIC VACUUM TO
HOOVER UP TACKS ETC.

SPECIAL HIGH-TECH
RADIO TRANSMITTER
AND RECEIVER

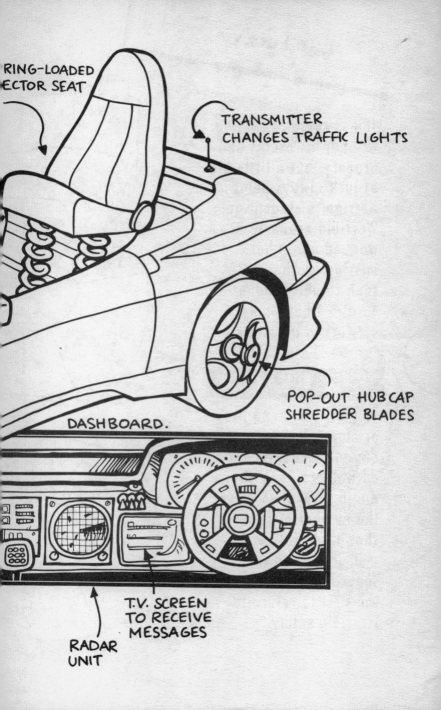

SPRING-LOADED
EJECTOR SEAT

TRANSMITTER
CHANGES TRAFFIC LIGHTS

POP-OUT HUB CAP
SHREDDER BLADES

DASHBOARD.

T.V. SCREEN
TO RECEIVE
MESSAGES

RADAR
UNIT

Get Lucky

James couldn't survive without his brains and bravery, but a little bit of luck always helps. Katrina, a student at Warfield Academy, is worried about her missing brother, last seen climbing Mount Jara in Tibet. James sets off to investigate.

ESCAPE FROM S.C.U.M.

To play, you need two or more players, one die and a counter for each player. Roll the die in turn, then move the number of squares shown and follow the instructions on the square. The winner is the first to return to Warfield safely.

MR MILBANKS' STUDY.

USE FLIGHT FACILITY ON MOUNTAIN BIKE MOVE FORWARD 3 SQUARES

BAR APP GO B SQU

FALLING ROCK BLOCKS PATH. GO BACK 3 SQUARES

USE CLIM ROPE MOVE FORW 2 SQ

TURN RAY TO SNOW USING I.Q.s MELTING DEVICE. MOVE FORWARD 3 SQUARES

DEAT DEVIC AIME JAM GO BA 5 SQ

SEND JAWS OVER MOUNTAIN EDGE. MOVE FORWARD 1 SQUARE

AVALA MISS G

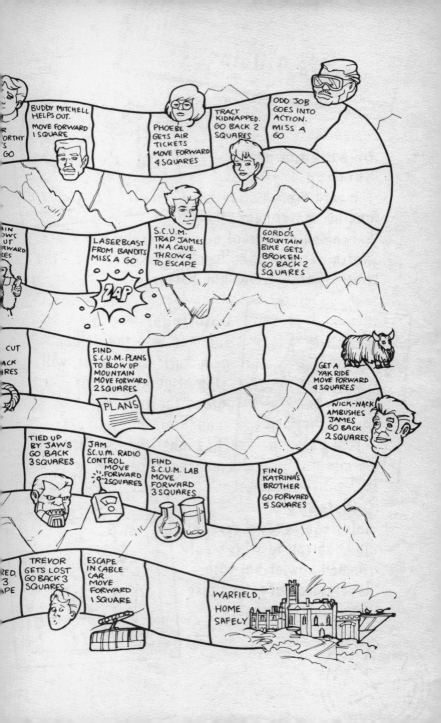

More Villains...

Dr Derange and Skullcap

The mad French scientist and his metal-headed

henchman are intent on evil 'research'. Watch out when Skullcap strokes his head - the static charge drives him berserk!

Goldfinger

The man with the golden gun, Auric Goldfinger, will stop at nothing in his greed for gold. His daughter, Goldiefinger, has inherited her father's penchant for gold.

Odd Job

Goldfinger's loyal servant, Odd Job can toss his steel-rimmed bowler hat with deadly accuracy. He's also a martial arts expert.

Baron Von Skarin

Illegal weapons dealer Baron Von Skarin lives in luxury in a Bavarian castle with his hulking pet wolf, Schnitzel, who can't wait to sink his teeth into James!

Ms Fortune

She's the richest, most poisonous woman in the world. A glamorous aristocrat, Ms Fortune dishes out the dirty work to her snooty butler, Snuffer.

25

Dr No

007's oldest and most troublesome enemy is an evil genius, and a cunning criminal. Now Dr No gloats in the trouble that he causes for James.

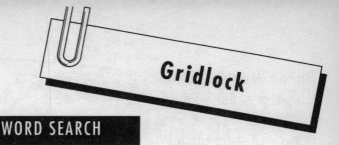

Gridlock

Can you find the characters hidden in the grid? They are all connected with James Bond Junior. The names may read forwards, backwards, up, down or diagonally. When you have found a name, draw a ring round it.

1. James
2. I.Q.
3. Tracy
4. Milbanks
5. Mitchell
6. Trevor
7. Gordo
8. Phoebe
9. Jaws
10. S.C.U.M. Lord
11. Nick Nack
12. Goldiefinger
13. Odd Job
14. Worm
15. Snuffer
16. Hotstones
17. Skullcap
18. Walker
D. Plank
19. Schnitzel
20. Von Skarin

26

A-MAZE-ING!

Von Skarin's favourite pet isn't the only risk James has to avoid to get out of the castle. Can you help him find the way and keep out of the Baron's nasty traps?

James' Hobbies

When he's not cracking crime or catching up on his studies under the watchful eye of Mr Milbanks, James knows how to enjoy himself. His hobbies often come in handy when he's out on assignment, too.

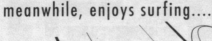

AIR, LAND AND WATER

As we know, James loves to drive a fast car — and he likes to pilot a plane, too. In more peaceful moments he glides above the rolling countryside around Warfield on the south coast of England.

Living on the coast means that James also gets the opportunity to try his skill at water sports. James' favourite is scuba-diving. Gordo, meanwhile, enjoys surfing....

Back on land, James' trusty mountain bike nips him down to Warfield village and back before Mr Milbanks has had time to blink.

Another of James' favourite hobbies is horseback riding. There's nothing James likes more than a gentle canter through the woods or a refreshing gallop in the field.

FANCY FOOTWORK

James enjoys a night out at the ballet, or watching Spanish flamenco dancers. But when it comes to taking to the dance floor himself, he prefers a slightly more modern style.

BOOKWORM BOND

In quieter moments, James likes to read. Books, magazines, newspapers, comic books - James finds them all full of fascinating and useful information that he often uses later on his missions.

Hidden Messages

HIEROGLYPHICS

As a spy, James must be prepared at all times. And that means swotting up on lots of different secret codes. Besides Morse Code and invisible writing, James is also skilled at deciphering ancient Egyptian hieroglyphs. You too can communicate in the language of the Pharaohs. Use the key to write your name in hieroglyphs, or write secret messages to your friends.

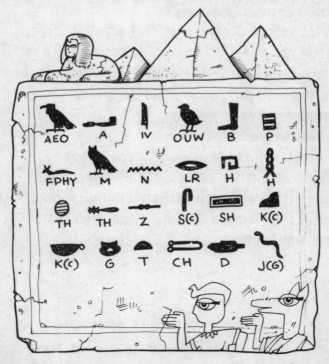

MIRROR WRITING

James' action packed life means he often has to communicate in a hurry. One of the simplest methods he uses to disguise messages from S.C.U.M. is to use mirror writing. Can you read the message below?

Around the World with James Bond Junior

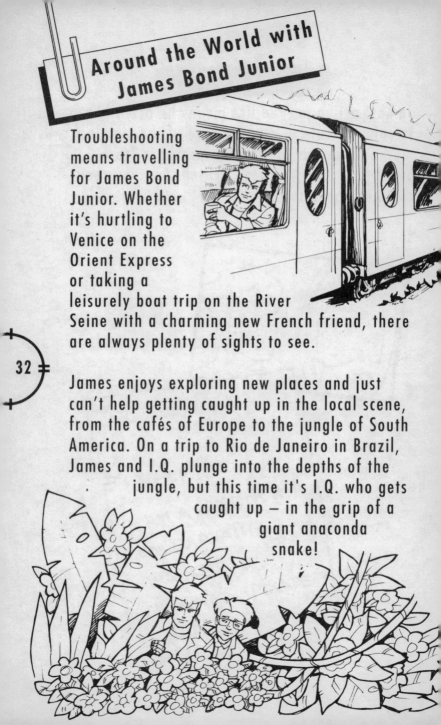

Troubleshooting means travelling for James Bond Junior. Whether it's hurtling to Venice on the Orient Express or taking a leisurely boat trip on the River Seine with a charming new French friend, there are always plenty of sights to see.

James enjoys exploring new places and just can't help getting caught up in the local scene, from the cafés of Europe to the jungle of South America. On a trip to Rio de Janeiro in Brazil, James and I.Q. plunge into the depths of the jungle, but this time it's I.Q. who gets caught up – in the grip of a giant anaconda snake!

James' globetrotting isn't all 20th century as he often combines his interest in history with his trips to foreign lands. On one of his missions, James must protect historic ruins from Worm, one of the slimiest members of S.C.U.M.

Of course, James also likes to relax on his travels. An island with plenty of sun, sand and surf means paradise to James and his friends. A holiday by the seaside also means that James can enjoy his favourite water sports in warmer climes!

It's certainly warm enough in Mexico, where James becomes embroiled in another devious S.C.U.M. plot. Ay caramba! Though travelling is always exciting, James is happy to return to Merry Olde England at the end of a trip.

Globetrotter's grammar

An undercover agent must blend in with the background. So when James is on assignment in far-flung places, that means being an expert in the local language. "My name is Bond-James Bond Junior" is James' favourite introduction. Can you guess which languages he is speaking in? The pictures are the clues, but in the wrong order!

1. Je m'appelle Bond, James Bond le jeune.
2. Ich heiße Bond, James Bond Junior.
3. Mi chiamo Bond, James Bond il giovane.
4. Me llamo Bond, James Bond menor.
5. Ya Bond, James Bond mladshy.
6. Ik heet Bond, James Bond Junior.

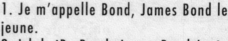

Even when he's over in the U.S.A., Bond has to watch his words. Because American English isn't quite the same as British English, it's easy for an English gent like James to get caught out as a Yankee impostor. Luckily, Gordo keeps him up to date with American vocabulary. Can you guess what Gordo means when he says the following?

1. Vacation
2. Cookies
3. Sneakers
4. Pants
5. Faucet
6. Chips
7. Subway
8. Trash
9. Allowance
10. Highway

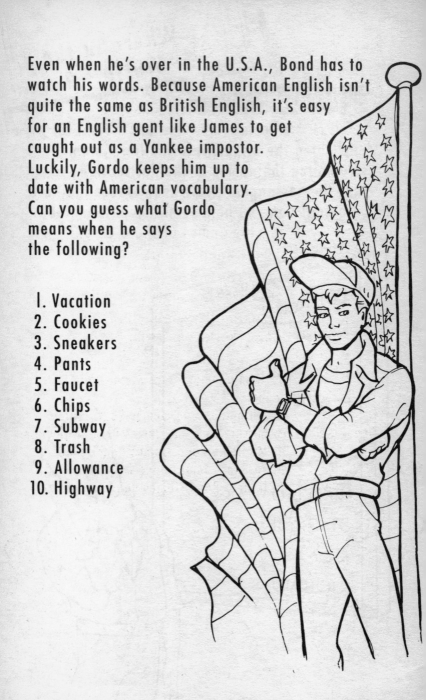

Where in the World...?

S.C.U.M. strikes again! This time they have infiltrated the airport information system, scrambling the names of the destinations so that the passengers don't know where they are going! Can you help James to unscramble the names of these cities?

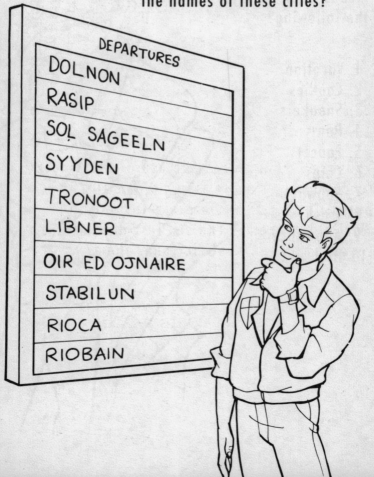

DEPARTURES

DOLNON

RASIP

SOL SAGEELN

SYYDEN

TRONOOT

LIBNER

OIR ED OJNAIRE

STABILUN

RIOCA

RIOBAIN

S.C.U.M. CHASE

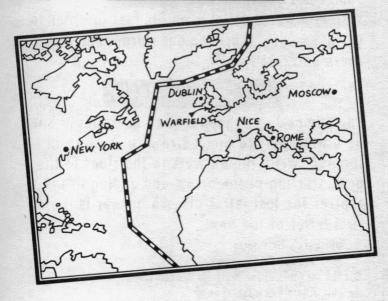

Thanks to Phoebe and the use of her credit cards, James flies to five major cities in pursuit of S.C.U.M. before returning to Warfield Academy. The six destinations are coded below. Can you decipher them?

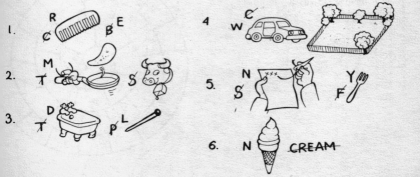

Playing with Words

James has got to be as fast with words as he is on his feet in order to catch S.C.U.M. Practise your wordpower with these quizzes:

CIRCLE QUIZ

Sometimes James goes around in circles – but he always gets to the centre of a mystery in the end. Write the answers to the clues in the grid, starting at the arrow and ending in the centre. The last letter of each answer is the first letter of the next.

1. Our hero's first name.
2. They are the No. 1 enemy.
3. The surname of the Warfield Academy headmaster.
4. This villain has a metal head.
5. Ms Farragut often helps James to finance his adventures.
6. Trevor's aristocratic father is an ____ .
7. Gordo's surname.
8. James travels to this South American city.
9. This villain uses his bowler hat as a weapon!
10. James's surname.

CROSS AN OLD ENEMY

Each clue below contains a word printed in CAPITAL letters. Write the opposite meaning in the numbered boxes. When read down the page, the first letter of each clue spells out the name of the oldest Bond enemy of them all!

1. James flies UP in his glider.
2. YOUNG Bond is 007's nephew.
3. James encounters HOT weather in Mexico.
4. Nick Nack has many FALSE disguises.
5. S.C.U.M. would like to get EVEN with James.
6. Phoebe is certainly not POOR.
7. Gordo is a NICE guy.
8. Warfield's gates are always CLOSED to intruders.

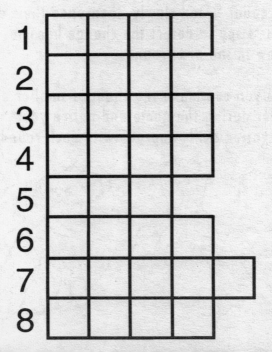

Skilful Spying

Sharpen your skills as a secret agent with these games of observation and detection.

WHAT DIFFERENCE?

Play this game with one or more friends. Choose one person to be the shadow and the others to be spies. While the shadow stands still, the spies study the shadow closely. Then the spies close their eyes and the shadow changes one thing about himself. He might untie a shoe, roll a sock down, or just uncross his arms or change the position of his feet. The spies count to ten slowly, then open their eyes. The first spy to detect the change becomes the shadow in the next round.

See if you can make the changes smaller and smaller during the game and notice your observation skills improve with each round.

ON THE TRAIL

Play this game with one or two friends. One person is the shadow, while the other person is the spy. The spy must follow the shadow without getting caught. When the shadow spins around, the spy must either hide or freeze in his place. The shadow scores if he sees the spy move. If he doesn't catch the spy, or the spy is hiding, then the spy scores a point. The first to score 10 wins the game.

If you have three players, the third is a counterspy who trails the spy. If the spy catches the counterspy moving, he scores one point. Otherwise, the counterspy scores. But the spy must not get caught by the shadow when he turns around to catch the counterspy.

SECURITY ALERT

If James misses his flight, his latest mission will be a failure. The last thing he needs is a delay at the security X-ray machine at the airport. Quickly, he empties his pockets.

42

Can you spot the 10 items that are missing from the contents of James' pockets? Spot the 10 missing items and James will catch his flight and prevent S.C.U.M.'s latest plot from succeeding!

S.C.U.M. QUIZ

To find out if you can become a member of the exclusive James Bond Junior Spy Network, see if you can answer the following questions. All the answers can be found in the book.

1. Where is Warfield Academy?
2. How old is James?
3. Who does James share a room with?
4. What liquid is used for invisible writing?
5. What do three short/three long/three short signals mean in Morse Code?
6. What does S.C.U.M. stand for?
7. Who is the shortest S.C.U.M. member?
8. What is the name of Von Skarin's pet wolf?

This is to certify that

- - - - - - - - - - - - - - - - - - -

is now a full member of the James Bond Junior Spy Network.

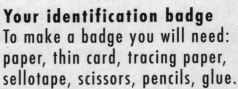

James Bond Junior Spy Network

James, I.Q., Tracy, Gordo, Phoebe, and even Trevor, all work together to help solve James' mysteries. Team up with your friends and be part of the James Bond Junior Spy Network.

You will need membership passports and badges. (Wear the badge on the inside of your clothing if you don't want anyone to know that you're a spy.)

Your identification badge

To make a badge you will need: paper, thin card, tracing paper, sellotape, scissors, pencils, glue.

1. Draw the James Bond Junior logo onto your piece of paper and colour it in. Cut around the circle.

2. Place the drawing on the card and draw another circle around it on the card.

3. Cut out the circle and glue your logo to the card.

4. Ask an adult to tape a safety pin to the back of your card.

5. Your ID badge is now ready!

The membership passport

To make a membership passport you will need:
a piece of A4 paper, scissors, a stapler, pens
and a photo-booth photo (optional).

1. Fold your piece of paper in half, then in half
and half again so that the paper is divided into
8 parts.

2. Cut the folded paper into 2
pieces along the centre fold.
You now have 2 booklets.

3. Secure the pages along the
folds with a stapler.

4. Cut along any unnecessary
folds so that you have 16
pages to your passport.

5. Draw the James Bond
Junior logo on the front of
the passport. If you have a

photo-booth picture of yourself, staple it inside
the book. Write your name and essential
details such as height, weight, colour of hair
and eyes. Don't let your
passport fall into the hands
of S.C.U.M. agents!

Enjoy the James Bond
Junior Spy Network!

PAGE 26

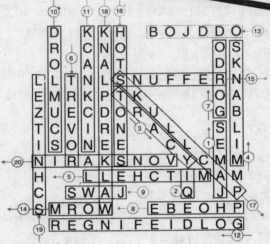

PAGE 31

The message reads:
HELP!! I AM A PRISONER ON
CAPTAIN WALKER D. PLANK'S
PIRATE SHIP

PAGE 34

1. French
2. German
3. Italian
4. Spanish
5. Russian
6. Dutch

PAGE 35

1. Holiday
2. Biscuits
3. Trainers
4. Trousers
5. Tap
6. Crisps
7. Underground train
8. Rubbish
9. Pocket money
10. Motorway

PAGE 36

London; Paris; Los Angeles;
Sydney; Toronto; Berlin;
Rio de Janeiro; Istanbul;
Cairo; Nairobi

PAGE 37

1. Rome
2. Moscow
3. Dublin
4. Warfield
5. New York
6. Nice

PAGE 38

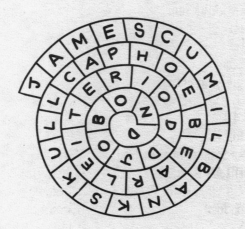

PAGE 39

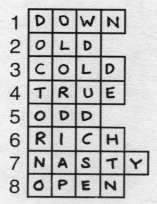

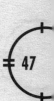

PAGE 42

The following objects are
missing from Picture B:
1. 20 pence piece
2. pen cap
3. one key
4. stamp
5. penknife
6. one stick of gum
7. sweet
8. ticket
9. notepad
10. magnifying glass

PAGE 43

SCUM QUIZ
1. On the South coast of England
2. Seventeen
3. I.Q.
4. Lemon Juice
5. S.O.S.
6. Saboteurs and Criminals United
in Mayhem.
7. Nick Nack
8. Schnitzel